**Disney · PIXAR**

# THE WORLD OF

## Cars

# *The Rookie*

Story retold by Kerry L. Bozza, Ed.D

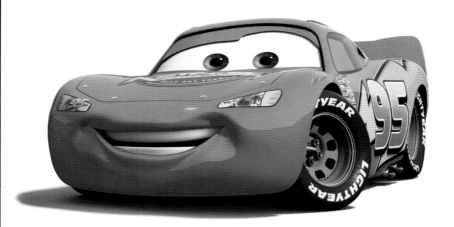

**Reader's Digest**
Children's Books®

Pleasantville, New York • Montréal, Québec • Bath, United Kingdom

*P**ound, pound, pound.* "Hey, Lightning, you ready?" yelled a voice through the trailer's door.

"Oh, yeah," said the hotshot red race car, Lightning McQueen, as he started to roll out of his trailer. "Lightning's ready." Then McQueen paused and looked up at the magnificent stadium. Cameras began to flash. Screams filled the air as thousands of race fans went crazy when they saw him. McQueen looked up and saw his picture on the huge video screen. He flashed the crowd a big smile. The fans cheered louder!

"Welcome to the Dinoco 400," shouted the announcer over the cheering crowd. Today was the last car race of the season. Three cars were tied for the season's points. The winner of today's race would win the Piston Cup! The Piston Cup was the biggest prize in racing. All the race cars wanted to be the one to win it.

Lightning McQueen wanted to win the Piston Cup as much as the rest of the cars. When McQueen had begun racing that season, no one had known who he was. But now, everyone knew him. He had a chance at becoming the first rookie to ever win the Piston Cup. But in order to do that, McQueen would have to beat The King—legendary racer Strip Weathers.

The King had won the Piston Cup four years in a row. But The King was retiring this

year and wanted to win the cup one last time. Since The King was retiring, the Dinoco Company would be looking for a new car to sponsor in the race. Whoever won this race was sure to be the next face of Dinoco, which meant fame and fortune. Winning this race meant everything.

The other racer that McQueen would have to beat was Chick Hicks. Chick had never won a Piston Cup. He had always come in second place. This year he was determined to come in first and would stop at nothing to do it.

Soon the race began. Cars were whipping around the track as fast as they could. Lap after lap, the legend, the runner-up, and the rookie battled for first place. As always, The King was in first place. And following close behind was Chick Hicks. Suddenly, however, McQueen punched the gas and overtook Chick. Angry, Chick roared up to McQueen and slammed into his rear corner, spinning McQueen into the infield. Chick laughed. But McQueen quickly recovered and made his way back to the track. Only now he was stuck at the back of the pack.

"Dinoco's all mine," sneered Chick at the other race cars. Then, in one sneaky turn of the

wheel, he slammed into the race car next to him, causing a huge wreck! "Get through *that*, McQueen!" laughed Chick over his bumper as he sped off into the lead.

Meanwhile McQueen, who was trailing safely behind the pack, watched as cars started smashing into the pileup. Quickly, he dodged the wreck by swerving to the left, then to the right, then back to the left, weaving in and out of the wrecked cars. Then, in one spectacular

and daring move, McQueen launched himself up and over the pile of cars. The crowd went wild and yelled his name. "Lightning!" they all cheered as he landed safely on all four wheels, back on track. Chick was furious!

Soon it was time for the race cars to pull into their pits to rotate their tires, check oil and water, and gas up. But McQueen kept going and took the lead!

As the laps began to tick off, McQueen realized that he had a huge lead over the other cars. So finally he decided to make a pit stop. His team began working.

"We need tires! Now!" yelled one of the pit crew workers.

"No, no tires! Just gas!" McQueen ordered his crew. As soon as the last drop of gas fell

into his tank, the rookie sped off. He still had on the old worn tires.

"What? You need tires!" his frustrated crew yelled after him.

But McQueen didn't care. He was almost a full lap ahead of the other cars and had only one lap left. He could taste victory.

"Checkered flag, here I come!" said McQueen confidently. But then…one of his rear tires blew.

*Ka-blam!*

"Oh, no!" yelled the announcer. "McQueen has blown a tire!"

Struggling, McQueen kept racing toward the finish line when…

*Ka-blam!* The second rear tire blew!

Behind him, McQueen heard the other cars zooming around the track, getting closer and closer. Pulling himself along, McQueen was determined to cross the line first.

"And down the stretch they come! And it's… And it's…!" shouted the announcer.

And just as The King and Chick crossed the finish line, McQueen slid forward in between the two cars. He had extended his tongue so far that it crossed the finish line

alongside the front ends of the two other racers. All three hit the finish line at the same time!

"It's too close to call!" shouted one of the announcers in disbelief.

"I don't believe it," laughed the other announcer. No one knew who had won the race. The judges told the three racers to hold tight while they reviewed the instant replay to determine the winner.

While they were waiting for the judges' decision, the press surrounded the cars. One reporter began to interview McQueen. While he spoke, McQueen's pit crew angrily began to replace his tires.

"McQueen, that was a risky move, not

taking tires," remarked the reporter. "Are you sorry you didn't have a crew chief out there?"

"No, I'm not," said McQueen. "cause I'm a one-man show!" Just then a camera started to take McQueen's picture, but a member of his pit crew was in the way.

McQueen yelled at the pit crew member to move. "Yo, Chuck!" yelled McQueen. "You're blocking the shot. Everyone wants to see 'the bolt.'"

"That's it! Come on, guys," ordered an angry member of the pit crew.

"Where are you going?" asked McQueen.

Hurt and angry, his crew decided to teach him a lesson. "We quit, Mr. One-Man Show!"

"Fine," McQueen replied with a laugh. Then he turned and began to pose again for the cameras. Suddenly, McQueen was surprised to find The King standing next to him.

"Hey, buddy, you're one gutsy racer," said The King as he approached the hotshot rookie. "But you're stupid," he quickly added.

"Excuse me?" asked McQueen.

"This ain't a one-man deal, kid. You need to wise up and get yourself a good crew chief and a good crew team," lectured the wise old race car. "You ain't gonna win unless you got good folks behind you."

McQueen nodded at The King, but he wasn't listening. Instead, he was watching the Dinoco helicopter as it landed behind the stage. Immediately, McQueen began dreaming of winning. In his dream he had already won the Piston Cup. Wearing the trademark Dinoco blue instead of red, McQueen saw himself standing with beautiful Dinoco showgirls at his side. He was being flown across the country by Dinoco helicopters. His picture was on the cover of every magazine because he was the star of his very own action adventure movie.

"*Ba-ba-ba-baa,*" interrupted the loud race horns. McQueen was jolted from his daydream by the sound.

"Ladies and gentlemen," announced one of the judges. "For the first time in Piston Cup history, we have…a three-way tie!"

McQueen was shocked—and embarrassed. He had been sure he had won and had burst through the banner onto the stage before the announcer finished speaking. He had been ready to take the stage by himself. Instead, McQueen was joined onstage by The King and Chick. The officials went on to say that a tiebreaker for the three racers would be held in California in one week.

"Hey, rook," challenged Chick. "First one to California gets Dinoco all to himself!"

"Oh, we'll see who gets there first, Chick," grumbled McQueen as he headed away from the crowd through the parked cars. Frustrated that he had not won, McQueen just wanted to get on the road. Finally he reached his parking space, but his driver, Mack, the loyal truck that pulled the trailer he rode in, was not there.

Just then, Mack appeared. "Hey kid! Congrats on the tie!" said Mack.

"I don't want to talk about it. Come on. Let's go, Mack," ordered McQueen. "Saddle up. What'd you do with my trailer?" Mack told McQueen that he had parked it over at the sponsor's tent.

*Shoot*, thought McQueen. He had hoped he

wouldn't have to make an appearance for his sponsor, Rust-eze. McQueen didn't like being sponsored by Rust-eze. He thought it wasn't very glamorous to be selling a product made for rusty bumpers!

Mack and McQueen drove up to the Rust-eze tent. McQueen peeked through the curtains and shuddered at what he saw. His sponsor's tent was filled with old cars. McQueen made a "yuck" face, like he was going to throw up. "*Ecck…*I hate rusty cars," said McQueen.

"They did give you your big break," Mack reminded him. "Besides, it's in your contract."

"Will you stop, please?" begged McQueen. "This is *not* good for my image," he muttered grumpily as he entered the tent.

"Hey, look! There he is!" his sponsor shouted excitedly. The cars in the tent spun around and began to rush up to McQueen. They all began to cheer and call out to him. "You're my hero, Mr. McQueen," called out a rusty car named Fred.

The rookie race car forced a smile. Slowly he climbed up onto the stage and gave a short

speech to the crowd. When he finished, the crowd went wild.

"We're looking forward to another great year—just like this year!" smiled his sponsors.

Smiling his best fake smile back at them, McQueen quickly rolled back into his trailer. When the door finally shut, McQueen dropped his fake smile.

After he won the race in California, he would have a new sponsor—Dinoco—and he would drop Rust-eze. McQueen wanted fancy tents and private helicopters, not medicated bumper ointment.

"California, here we come!" shouted Mack through the intercom as he pulled out onto the highway.

"Dinoco, here we come," McQueen quietly whispered to himself.